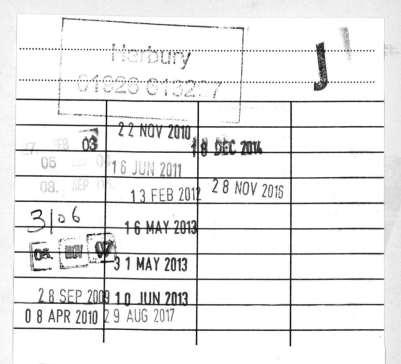

Some other books by Margaret Ryan . . .

Hover Boy:
1: Fizzy Feet
3: Missing Moggy Mystery

For younger readers . . .

The Canterbury Tales
1: The Big Sister's Tale
2: The Little Brother's Tale
3: The Little Sister's Tale

For older readers . . .

Operation Boyfriend

published by Hodder Children's Books

BEAT THE BULLY

MARGARET RYAN

ILLUSTRATED BY NICOLA SLATER

Hodder
Children's
Books

a division of Hodder Headline Limited

For Viv, with love –
Margaret Ryan

Text copyright © 2002 Margaret Ryan
Illustrations copyright © 2002 Nicola Slater

First published in Great Britain in 2002
by Hodder Children's Books

10 9 8 7 6 5 4 3 2 1

A Catalogue record for this book is available from the British Library

ISBN 0 340 80605 2

Printed and bound in Great Britain by
Bookmarque Ltd, Croydon, Surrey

Hodder Children's Books
A division of Hodder Headline Limited
338 Euston Road, London NW1 3BH

CHAPTER ONE

Some people are born with a special gift. Like being able to play the trombone aged two-and-a-half, or being able to do hard sums without using their fingers. Oscar Smith was born with a special gift. He wasn't musical or mathematical, but he could hover. Three feet up in the air.

He was three feet up in the air now looking out of the sitting-room window at the rain.

"I'm bored," he said. "I don't want a Monday holiday from school. I like school, now that I'm going to the School Of Greatly Gifted Youth. It is a bit of a mouthful, though. No wonder they call it S.O.G.G.Y. for short."

Suddenly the faint feeling of fizziness in his feet grew stronger, and he rose even higher. It was still raining outside, he was still bored, but now he was bored three-and-a-half-feet up in the air.

"I've got nothing to do," he said to his mum, who was busy hoovering the sitting-room carpet.

"You could clean that light shade while you're up in the air," she said, and handed him a duster.

"I bet this never happened to Superman," Oscar muttered.

That gave him an idea. He hummed the Superman theme tune, and threw his arms in the air. THUD! He cracked his knuckles on the ceiling and banged his nose on the light shade.

"Plonker," said Evie, one of Oscar's twin sisters. "I hope you're not going to be hovering around all day doing stupid things, and getting in our way. Angie and I are going to have our beauty school in here. We've got our green beauty masks and our nail polish and the orange streaks for our hair all ready."

"Orange streaks," said Oscar, "with pink hair! Won't that look a bit odd?"

"Huh, *you* should talk. At least we don't hover in the air half the time. You only do it to get out of the washing up."

"Don't," said Oscar.

"Do," said the twins.

"Do be quiet, you lot," said their mum. "Oscar, why don't you invite Gnatalie and Wibbly round for the day. You can have the old caravan in the back garden as your den and that'll keep you out of everyone's hair."

"Especially pink hair with orange streaks," grinned Oscar.

Gnatalie and Wibbly were Oscar's best friends at S.O.G.G.Y. Gnatalie's great gift was x-ray vision. When she tried really hard she could see through anything; doors, walls and windows, naturally.

Wibbly's great gift was mind-reading. If he tried really hard he could tell what people were thinking almost before they knew themselves.

Oscar's great gift was hovering, of course. At his last school he had tried to hide his hovering. He didn't want to be thought odd or strange or weird. It had caused upset at home too. One minute his parents thought they had an ordinary son, and the next they found him hovering three feet in the air. They had blamed each other.

"It must come from your side of the family," said his dad to his mum. "We're all perfectly normal."

"There's nothing wrong with *my* family," bristled his mum. "What about your Great Aunt Nellie? Wasn't she a belly dancer?"

Oscar's twin sisters had been furious.

"He's only doing it to get attention," they said. "He's just a show-off!"

In the end, the family told no one, hoping Oscar's hovering would go away as quickly as it had come. But it hadn't.

Oscar hovered over to the phone to call his friends, but just as he got there, the faint feeling of fizziness in his feet disappeared, and he came down with a clatter, and knocked over the phone table.

"Clumsy clogs," muttered Evie, sweeping past.

"Weirdo," added Angie, tripping over him.

Oscar said nothing. He was used to it. He picked himself up from the carpet, rubbed his rear end, and dialled Gnatalie's number.

The phone at the other end rang three times, then the answering machine clicked on.

"You have reached the studios of the famous sculptors, Mario and Marianne. We're too busy creating wonderful sculptures to talk to you right now, but if you want to

leave a message, please do so after the tinkling tone, and we'll get back to you some time in the future. Probably."

"Oh no," Oscar muttered. "Gnatalie must be out, and her parents never answer the telephone."

He was just about to put the phone down when he heard Gnatalie's voice.

"Hullo, hullo. Who is it? Are you still there?"

"Hi, Gnatalie," said Oscar. "It's me. I thought you were out."

"I was," said Gnatalie. "I went shopping for some food. Mum and Dad are often too busy to eat, or else they just forget."

"I know," said Oscar. He had met Gnatalie's mum and dad. They were nice, although they couldn't spell, and didn't wash very often. They made sculptures out of anything they could find. Their bathroom door had gone

11

into a sculpture and Gnatalie had to stay in the bath once for three hours to save it from disappearing too.

"I wondered if you'd like to come over for the day," said Oscar. "Mum says we can have the old caravan in the back garden as a den."

"Cool," said Gnatalie. "I'll be there in ten minutes, once I've hidden the food. I don't want my fish fingers disappearing into a sculpture."

"OK," grinned Oscar. "I'll phone Wibbly, too."

Wibbly was delighted to come round. "It'll get me out of chopping veggies. Mum's making something called Purple Aubergine Surprise. It'll be a surprise if it's edible."

Oscar smiled. Wibbly's mum made exotic casseroles for a living. Trouble was, Wibbly had to eat the leftovers in his school sandwiches or for tea.

Trouble with *that* was his favourite
tea was sausage and chips. Sometimes
Oscar felt his parents were a bit
ordinary compared to Gnatalie's
and Wibbly's, but at least they
remembered to feed him regularly
and he did get sausage and chips.

Oscar gathered up some cushions
and crisps and chocolate biscuits and
ran out into the back garden. He
wished he were skinny enough to
dodge between the fat raindrops that
soaked him before he reached the old
caravan. It hadn't been used for ages
and smelt of damp and next door's cat.
Oscar's dad used to tow the caravan to
the seaside on family holidays till the
twins insisted on going abroad.

Oscar spread out the cushions then
looked in the cupboard where they had
kept all the holiday games and puzzles,
but he couldn't find the dice for the

games, and the jigsaws all had pieces missing. He dived under a storage area and had practically disappeared into it when the door opened and Gnatalie and Wibbly came in.

"Oh look, it's Hover Bum," they grinned.

Red-faced, Oscar stood up. "I was looking for bits of jigsaw."

Gnatalie screwed up her eyes
and looked through the side of the
storage area.

"There's an old sock and a
broken Game Boy in there," she
said. "But no jigsaw bits."

"I don't like jigsaws anyway,"
said Wibbly. "My mum's got one
of a million baked beans. Gives me
wind just to look at it."

Gnatalie giggled. "I brought us
some food."

"So did I," said Wibbly.

"Me too," grinned Oscar. "So what
do you think of this place as a den?"

"Cool," said Wibbly. "I've never been
in a caravan before."

"Me neither," said Gnatalie. "Shall
I make us a sign that says 'Private den
– Keep out'?"

The boys nodded. Gnatalie
straightened out an empty cereal

box, found an old felt-tip pen and wrote, "Privit din – ceep out."

"There now. What do you think of that?" she said.

Oscar and Wibbly looked at Gnatalie's beaming face.

"It's great," they said. "Hang it out now."

The sign was hardly up on the door when Evie and Angie appeared. They had the sign in their hands.

"'Privit din'?" they said. "'*Privit din*'! Who's the rotten speller?"

Gnatalie blushed scarlet. "Me," she mumbled. "I'm not very good at spelling."

"Obviously," said the twins. "We won the spelling competition in our school last year. Although *we* just go to an *ordinary* school. We don't go to a fancy school for children with special gifts. You do and you can't even spell."

"But Gnatalie has x-ray vision," said Oscar. "That's really special."

"OK," challenged the twins. "Tell us what we had for breakfast, if you can!"

Gnatalie screwed up her eyes and looked into the twins' rounded tums.

"Not easy to be sure," she said. "But it looks like it might have been pancakes and syrup."

"Pancakes and syrup!" yelled Oscar. "You pair of greedy guts. You told me there was none left. I had to have old burnt toast instead." And the faint feeling of fizziness in his feet started, and he shot three feet up into the air, and banged his head on the ceiling. Then he hovered towards the twins. Evie and Angie left hurriedly, slamming the caravan door behind them.

"Greedy guts," muttered Oscar

again, and hovered back from the door.

He was just coming slowly down to earth again when he noticed an old newspaper on the bookshelf. It was dated 6 October, the same day and year as his birthday. He glanced through it and something else caught his eye.

"Look at this," he said to Gnatalie and Wibbly.

Gnatalie looked and read: "'Goat for sale. Eats anything. Very fond of children.'"

"Above that," said Oscar.

"'Little red rooster. Free to good home. New owners must be vegetarian,'" read Wibbly.

"Above that," sighed Oscar. "Look! Unidentified flying object seen above Bradshaw maternity hospital on 6 October in the year that I was born. The U.F.O. was reported by Madame E. Carella. That's Madame Estella, our head teacher, I'm sure of it."

Oscar glanced back at the paper. "But it says here no on else sighted the U.F.O. and the police say it was more than likely a low-flying plane. They obviously thought Madame Estella was as nutty as a fruitcake."

"Or daft as a brush," said Gnatalie.

"Or as screwy as a screwy thing you take out corks with," said Wibbly.

"Which she's not," said Oscar. "She's a little bit odd, but at S.O.G.G.Y. we're all a little bit odd!" He looked out of the caravan window into the pouring rain. "There's not a lot else we can do today," he said, "so why don't we go and ask mum if we can visit Madame Estella and get her to tell us more about the U.F.O."

CHAPTER TWO

Madame Estella lived in a little cottage in the grounds of the School Of Greatly Gifted Youth, so Oscar, Gnatalie and Wibbly caught the number nine bus outside Oscar's house, and squeezed into one seat at the back.

The bus driver eyed them suspiciously. They gave her their wide-eyed, innocent look, and she started up the bus. Unfortunately, the faint feeling of fizziness started up in Oscar's feet when they were only halfway to the school. "Oh no," he said, and started to rise up into the air.

"Don't worry," said Gnatalie, and

she and Wibbly sat on him to stop
his head hitting the roof.

Unfortunately, the bus driver
thought they were messing about, and
put them off two stops too soon, and
they had to walk the rest of the way.

They were very wet when they
reached Madame Estella's cottage.
The cottage, like the school, was old
and crumbling, held together by the
ivy that clung to the walls. But there was
a light on in the sitting-room and the
cottage door opened in welcome
as they trudged up the path.

"Hullo, my dears," said Madame
Estella. "I've been expecting you.
I had a feeling I would have visitors
today. But, just look at you. You're
soaked through. Come in. Come in."

She took their wet anoraks and
placed them by the kitchen fire,
then she shooed the friends into

the tiny sitting-room.

"Sit where you can, she said. "I'm so sorry about the mess."

The room was covered in dust sheets. The dust sheets were covered in paint. So was Madame Estella. Her long white smock had splodges of colour everywhere. Somehow it suited her. As usual, her hair was piled up on top of her head, and sticking out of it were two slim paint-brushes and a pencil.

"It was such a wet day I decided to cheer myself up by painting the ceiling," she said.

Oscar, Gnatalie and Wibbly looked up. The ceiling was a deep, mysterious blue, and dotted all over it were tiny silver stars and red and yellow whirling planets.

"Wow," cried the three friends. "Awesome."

"I'm so glad you like it," beamed
Madame Estella. "But it's taking me
ages, and I keep getting a crick in
my neck looking upwards."

Oscar felt the faint feeling of
fizziness start in his feet again, and
he smiled as he rose gently into the
air. He plucked a paint-brush from
Madame Estella's hair.

23

"I can easily do some of these for you," he said, and began painting silver stars. This was much more fun than dusting light shades.

"Oh, how wonderful, Oscar," she said. "Now, just let me get you some lemonade and cookies, and you can tell me what's brought you here." And she disappeared into the kitchen.

Two minutes later she was back, carrying a tray of lemonade and cookies. Following close behind was her cat, Mystic Mog. Mystic Mog gave the three friends a long cool look then seated herself expectantly at Madame Estella's feet.

Suddenly the faint feeling of fizziness in Oscar's feet went away, and he dropped down from the ceiling. He nearly landed on the cat, but she didn't leap away. Instead she just sat there, blinking at Oscar. Oscar reached out and stroked her soft fur.

"Sorry, Mystic Mog," he said. "Hope I didn't frighten you."

And, just for a moment, Oscar was almost sure he heard the cat say, "Not at all, Oscar."

Oscar blinked at Mystic Mog. Mystic Mog blinked back. Madame Estella looked anxiously at the two of them. Then . . .

"Who likes chocolate cookies?" she asked brightly.

They all did. Especially Mystic Mog. She kept her eyes on Oscar's face and nibbled daintily.

Oscar shook his head. Of course the cat hadn't spoken. Cats *miaow*. Cats *purr*. Cats *hiss* when they're angry. Cats don't speak. Wibbly looked at Oscar and read his mind. He raised an eyebrow. Oscar shrugged his shoulders and shook his head. Gnatalie looked at

25

the pair of them. What was all this eyebrow raising and shoulder shrugging? *What* was going on?

"Now," said Madame Estella. "Tell me why you're here, or is this just a social call? Either way I'm delighted to see you."

"We wondered," said Oscar, taking the old newspaper out of his pocket, "if you could tell us a little more about this. I found the newspaper in our caravan and read the item about the U.F.O. you spotted. You see I was born that same night in Bradshaw maternity hospital."

"I see," said Madame Estella, feeding Mystic Mog more cookie crumbs. "Well, there's not much more to tell really. I was living in the big house then with the other teachers. Before I made it into a school, S.O.G.G.Y. was a sanctuary for anyone with a special gift. The world can be a very cruel place for anyone who is slightly different."

The children nodded.

"I remember it was a fine night. Cold and clear. I like to take a little walk before bedtime and look at the stars. I was just passing the hospital when I saw a circle of green lights appear. They hovered over the hospital roof. I didn't know what they were, but I stopped and watched them. Then the lights disappeared as quickly as they'd come, and that was that. I reported it to the police, but as usual, they thought I was mad and said it was probably a low-flying plane."

"*As usual?*" said Oscar. "You mean you've reported this kind of thing before?"

"Several times. But always with the same result. Maybe I am mad.

27

Maybe I *do* see things. I've got all the cuttings from the local paper if you want to see them."

"Yes, please," said Oscar.

Madame Estella threw back a dust sheet and uncovered a chest of drawers. She pulled open the top drawer and brought out a scrapbook. Carefully stuck inside were several newspaper clippings.

"That's funny. Here's a sighting on the same day that I was born," said Gnatalie.

"And here's one on my birthday too," said Wibbly.

"I wonder if all cuttings match up with the birthdays of the children in the school?" said Oscar.

Madame Estella looked at Oscar in surprise. "I hadn't thought of that," she said. "That's something I can check when I go into school tomorrow.

In the meantime, have some more cookies. There's plenty left."

Oscar had just bitten thoughtfully into his fourth cookie when Mystic Mog surprised him by jumping up on to his chair and walking round behind him.

She nuzzled his ear with her delicate little nose, and her whiskers tickled his cheek. But that wasn't all. Once again Oscar was almost certain he heard her speak. He was almost sure he heard her whisper, "Well done, Hover Boy."

But he couldn't have, could he? He looked over at Wibbly. Wibbly frowned and raised both eyebrows.

Gnatalie looked at the pair of them. Something was definitely up.

The rain had gone by the time they said goodbye to Madame Estella, but, as soon as they reached the front gate Gnatalie said, "OK, you two, what was going on in there? What was that shrugging of shoulders and raising of eyebrows all about. Did I miss something?"

"Oh, I expect it's nothing," said Oscar. "I expect I imagined it."

"Imagined what?"

"That he heard Mystic Mog speak," said Wibbly, "I read his mind back there."

"But cats can't speak," said Gnatalie. "They don't have right kind of voice box or something."

"I know," said Oscar. "But boys don't hover either, do they?"

They splashed home, through
every puddle they could find and
arrived back at their den. They
had just squelched out of their shoes
when Evie and Angie burst in.

"Well," they said. "Notice anything
different about us?"

Gnatalie looked hard at the twins.
"You're not wearing matching
T-shirts?"

31

"Don't be stupid. That's for kids."

Wibbly looked hard at the twins. "You're wearing odd socks."

"That's the latest fashion statement. Don't you know anything?"

Oscar looked hard at his two sisters. Then he remembered about the beauty school.

"I know," he said. "You've made yourselves even more beautiful."

Evie and Angie ran their newly-polished nails through their newly-streaked orange hair.

"But when," grinned Oscar, "will you take off the green beauty mask?"

"It is off," screeched the twins and ran to look in the mirror. "It's guaranteed to make you more beautiful than ever."

"Better ask for your money back then," said Oscar. "It obviously didn't work."

CHAPTER THREE

Oscar got up early for school next
morning. He had recently started
doing this, for three reasons . . .
1. Getting up early meant he didn't
have to have a cold shower – the twins
always used up all the hot water.
2. He could get a decent breakfast – the
twins always scoffed everything in sight.
3. He had time to walk to school –
the twins always complained when he
stood at the bus stop with them. They
didn't like him around when their
friends were there.

Oscar smiled at his sleepy reflection
in the mirror. It was great being Hover

Boy. It was great having a special gift now that he was going to S.O.G.G.Y. No one there thought he was weird. Everyone there had a special gift, well, nearly everyone.

Oscar had a hot shower, carefully looking for a shampoo that wouldn't turn his hair pink or orange. Then he had his favourite breakfast of toast and chocolate spread, and set off for school.

It was a cold, windy morning and people scurried past with their coat collars turned up, so no one seemed to notice the freckle-faced boy who sometimes walked and sometimes hovered along the road to school.

As usual, Oscar smiled as he rounded the corner of Beacham Road and caught sight of S.O.G.G.Y. He didn't think it looked like a proper school at all. It was a large crumbly old

house set well back from the road
behind creaky high gates. Its chimney
pots were set at a rakish angle and curls
of smoke suggested that Mr Periwinkle,
the caretaker, had already been busy
stoking the old boiler.

The house had once been owned by
wealthy ancestors of Madame Estella,
who'd had plenty of servants to look
after them. There were little bells to call

for the servants whenever a cup of tea or coffee was required.

The bells didn't work now, neither did the gates which sagged badly on their hinges. The garden was wild and overgrown and there was a nasty patch of brambles at the side of the house that could rip socks and ankles if you weren't careful.

Oscar, Gnatalie and Wibbly knew a secret path round the brambles, though, and had their own special place on the other side where they met at break and at lunchtime. An old oak tree had blown down there and was a great place to sit and have a chat. Oscar loved it. He loved everything about S.O.G.G.Y. Well, almost everything.

He wasn't very keen on Banger McGrath, the head boy. He bullied everyone and stole their sweets. He always liked to be the centre of attention

and get his own way. Banger's father
now owned the school, so Banger
thought he could get away with
anything. He thought he was really
special. In fact, he had no special gifts at
all, and was at the school to try to learn
some. His father hoped the school
would one day make him lots of money.

Oscar went through the creaky
gates and walked up the worn steps
into the school. As usual, Mystic Mog
was sitting on the top step.

Oscar stooped to stroke her silky
head. Had she spoken to him yesterday?

"Morning Mog," he said.

Mystic Mog blinked and Oscar was
almost sure he heard her say, "Good
morning, Oscar," but a fire engine was
passing at that moment and he couldn't
be completely certain.

Mystic Mog went back to cleaning
her paws and Oscar headed into school.

He wandered through the many narrow passageways to his classroom and found Gnatalie and Wibbly already there. They were early birds too.

"Hi, Hover Boy," said Gnatalie. "I was just telling Wibbly about Mum and Dad's latest idea for sculpture. It's called Takeaways and is to be made of lots of used takeaway cartons, so we're having to eat plenty of pizza and curries and chicken chow mein. It's wonderful. Want to come to my house for tea tonight? You can have anything you like so long as it's a takeaway."

"I'll have a pepperoni pizza," grinned Oscar.

"Can I have fish and chips? It's my favourite next to sausage and chips," said Wibbly.

At that moment the classroom door opened and Madame Estella came in, carrying the school register. She wore a

long blue dress that shimmered as she
moved and her hair was piled up high
on top of her head. It looked even more
higgledy-piggledly than normal. As well
as the usual pens and pencils stuck in
her hair Oscar spotted a toothbrush.

Madame Estella's eyes were shining.
"You were right about the U.F.O.
sightings, Oscar," she said. "Just look
at the register." Beside the pupils'
names she had placed a small red cross.
"The dates of my sightings are exactly
the same as these birth dates," she said.
"That's all the pupils in the school
except one. There's only one birthday
that doesn't fit . . ."

Oscar already knew who that was.

"Banger McGrath," he said.

Madame Estella nodded.

"But what does it all mean?" asked
Oscar. "Have our special gifts been
given to us by aliens? And if so, why?"

39

CHAPTER FOUR

Banger McGrath hadn't enjoyed his Monday holiday from school. He'd wanted to spend the day playing games on his computer. He already had all his favourite food and drink piled up beside it and was just about to start on his favourite game when his dad came into the room.

His dad was a big man, built like a bouncer, with a beef tomato for a face. On his right pinkie he wore a large gold ring with his initials – "B.M." – engraved on it. A large gold watch, which showed the time in all the world's capitals, dug into the flesh of

his left wrist, while on his right hung
a gold bracelet heavy enough to buy a
small country. To add to his glitter he
had a gold front tooth with a diamond
in it. It sparkled when he spoke.

"Boris Junior!" he roared.

"Whaaaaat?" said Banger, who hated
being called Boris Junior.

"Just what do you think you're doing?"

"Just playing, Dad," said Banger.

"Playing? *Playing?* Why aren't you working? Why aren't you doing your homework? Why aren't you practising these special gifts they're supposed to be teaching you at that S.O.G.G.Y. place?"

"It's a holiday, Dad, and I haven't got any homework."

"What about the special gifts, then? You should be working on them. You'll never get anywhere without working, boy. Just look at me. You don't think I got where I am today without working?"

"No, Dad," said Banger.

"You don't think I got to own half the town without working?"

"No, Dad."

"You don't think I was able to buy that crumbly old school of yours from that crazy head teacher without working?"

"No, Dad."

"Not that I paid a lot for it. Tricked

the silly woman good and proper,
I did. But that's another story. Now
then, show me what special gifts
you've learned."

"Er, well, I haven't really learned
any yet, Dad."

"Nonsense, you must have learned
something from *someone*. What about
that girl with the green fingers you sit
beside? What's her name? Bendy
Wendy."

"Wanda Fonda," said Banger.

"That's her. Can't she grow things
just by looking at them?"

"Yes," said Banger and touched
his nose. It was as well not to annoy
Wanda. He hadn't enjoyed being
called Pinocchio for a day. Anyway *he*
was supposed to be the one that
called people names.

"Well," said Banger's dad. "Didn't
she show you what to do?"

"Yes," said Banger. "She showed me how to make a plant grow just by staring at it."

"Wonderful," said his dad. "There's a lot of money to be made from growing plants. Just think of all the gardening programmes on television. You could be on one of those. You could have your own show. We've got a plant in the hall. Go and fetch it right now."

Banger trailed into the hall and staggered back with a huge rubber plant in a terracotta pot.

"Right," said his dad. "Now what did Wanda Fonda tell you to do?"

"Just stare at it, Dad, and say, 'GROW, PLANT, GROW.'"

"Right then. Go on. Show me."

Banger stared at the plant. Its leaves were a glossy dark green, and silvery grey-green moss covered the top of the pot.

"Grow, plant, grow," muttered Banger.
Nothing happened.

"You'll have to stare harder and say the words louder," said his dad.

Banger screwed up his eyes and stared harder. "Grow, plant, grow," he said, louder.

Still nothing happened. The plant stayed exactly the same size.

"Keep working at it, Boris Junior.
"I didn't get where I am today without working at it. And shout louder. Perhaps

the plant's deaf. I want to be able to hear you at the other end of the house."

Banger stared and shouted till he was red in the face, but still the plant refused to grow. It was only when his eyes were watering from staring and his throat was hoarse from shouting that he noticed a little label in among the leaves of the plant. He pulled it out and read, "Everlasting plant – do not water."

"Oh, no," groaned Banger and kicked the plant across the floor.

"What's all this?" said his dad, coming to find out why the shouting had stopped.

Banger showed him the label.

"Idiot boy," he said. "You should have noticed that in the first place. Wait a minute, what about this new boy that's come to the school? What's his name . . . Hover Boy. Perhaps

you'll have more success learning
from him. Imagine if you could
hover, Boris Junior. That would be
a real gift to have. You could be the
next Batman or Superman and I
could make a fortune. Can't
understand that boy's parents not
wanting to make money out of him.
Must be barmy.

"Right, forget the plant growing,
from now on I want you to stick to
Hover Boy like glue. Watch everything
he does and *learn, learn, learn*. I want
you to have a special gift very soon.
If I don't see a return on my money
I'll close that school down and build
a block of flats. Understand?"

CHAPTER FIVE

Suddenly Oscar couldn't get rid of
Banger. He'd started to be a real
problem. He never let Oscar out of
his sight. If Oscar walked, Banger
walked. If Oscar ran, Banger ran.
Wherever Oscar went, Banger went
too. Whenever Oscar spoke to Gnatalie
or Wibbly, Banger would pop up in
between them saying . . .

"What are you talking about? Is it
about your special gifts? Is it about me?
I want to hear."

He was even worse when Oscar's
hovering came on. Banger started lying
on the ground under Oscar's feet,

looking up at them as if staring at the soles of his trainers would tell him something. Even when Oscar fell down on top of him he still carried on.

"Go away, Banger," said Oscar. "Go away and annoy someone else. Why are you behaving like this?"

"I want to find out your secret, Oscar Smith. I want to find out the secret of your hovering. I want to be able to do it. I want to have some special gifts – or else."

"Or else what?" Oscar frowned.

"Or else my dad says he'll close down the school and build a block of flats, so there!"

"Close down S.O.G.G.Y.?" cried Oscar. "He can't do that!"

"Oh yes, he can," sneered Banger. "My dad can do anything."

Oscar felt his throat go dry and a sick feeling start in the pit of his stomach.

Banger was right. His dad *could* close down the school. But he couldn't let that happen. He mustn't let that happen. He must stop it at all costs. But how? Oscar nibbled a fingernail and worried.

The first discovery that day was Maths. Not one of Oscar's favourite lessons. Even calling it a discovery instead of a lesson didn't make it any better, or any easier. Besides, Oscar's mind was on higher things: how to save the school. He just had to get away from Banger long enough to tell Gnatalie and Wibbly what had happened.

"Oscar Smith," said Miss Twitching, who could do really complicated sums in her head, "I don't seem to have your full attention today. In fact, I don't seem to have your attention at all. Don't you find long division totally fascinating?"

"No, I mean yes, I mean—"

"Then come and work out this example for us on the blackboard."

Red-faced, Oscar went out to the blackboard. It was covered in numbers. He looked at them in despair. He hadn't a clue what they meant. He took the chalk from Miss Twitching and put on what he hoped was an intelligent expression. He was just going to try out a two or maybe a three on the blackboard when he felt the faint fizziness in his feet. He slowly rose up into the air.

The class giggled.

Miss Twitching sighed and pushed up the blackboard till the long division sum was level with Oscar. Oscar thought about the sum again. He was just going to try out a five or a six on the blackboard when the faint feeling of fizziness went away again and he slowly sank to the floor.

The class laughed out loud.

Miss Twitching blew down through her nose and tapped her foot like an impatient horse, and pulled the board down again. The faint feeling of fizziness returned to Oscar's feet and he rose slowly into the air once more.

The class rolled about clutching their sides.

"Oscar Smith," said Miss Twitching, "are you doing that on purpose?"

"No, Miss Twitching. I can't control it yet. It just happens."

"Well, it also just happens that you will do six extra long division sums for homework tonight, and more if you don't pay attention for the rest of this discovery. Do you understand?"

"Yes, Miss Twitching," sighed Oscar and hovered back to his seat. It was five more minutes before the faint feeling of fizziness went away and he could sit down.

"That was brilliant, Oscar," said Gnatalie at the end of the discovery. "Best Maths discovery we've ever had."

"Yes, but not for me," said Oscar. "Have you ever tried writing in your Maths book three feet up in the air? And I've got extra homework."

"I'll help you," said Wibbly. "I'm

quite good at Maths. It's having to work out all the quantities for Mum and her exotic casseroles. She just throws in a handful of this and a dollop of that, but you can't write that in a recipe book!"

"I don't know what your mum would do without you, Wibbly," said Gnatalie.

Wibbly blushed. "No, neither do I."

"Listen," whispered Oscar. "There's something important I have to talk to you about. But not here." And he nodded at Banger who was heading in their direction. "Meet me in the usual place at break."

CHAPTER SIX

Oscar nearly didn't make it to the secret meeting place. During break Banger followed him all round the school grounds. If Oscar hopped, Banger hopped. If Oscar jumped, Banger jumped. If Oscar stopped suddenly, Banger bumped into him. He was closer than a shadow. Fortunately Mr Periwinkle came looking for Banger and made him give back a football he'd taken from one of the other children. Oscar saw his chance and slipped away taking the secret path round the bramble patch to their meeting place.

"Hi, Oscar. We thought you'd got

lost," said Gnatalie.

"I wish Banger would get lost," muttered Oscar. "He's following me around like a bad smell, but that's not what I wanted to talk to you about." And he told them about Banger's dad's threat to close the school.

"But he can't," gasped Gnatalie and Wibbly.

"He can," said Oscar. "That's why we have to think up ways to stop him, but there's isn't enough time to talk about it now."

"And we can't talk at the next discovery either," said Wibbly. "It's Extra-acute hearing."

"What?" said Oscar.

"Extra-acute hearing."

"Pardon?" said Oscar.

"Extra – oh very funny, Hover Boy," grinned Wibbly. "I bet you're no good at it."

*   *   *

Mr Grassgrow took the Extra-acute hearing discovery, and Oscar watched, fascinated, as Peter Purbright, star of that class, showed everyone his special gift.

"Now, Peter," beamed Mr Grassgrow. "I have arranged with Madame Estella that at exactly eleven o'clock she will be sitting at her desk, in her room, at the other end of the school and will recite a short poem. Let's see if you can hear it. Now, who has the correct time? My watch has stopped."

"Three minutes and thirty-one seconds to eleven," shouted out Banger McGrath. "It says so on my new super de luxe multi-functional space-age time piece. And it's never wrong."

"Actually," said Oscar. "That's the town hall clock striking eleven now."

Everyone listened. Sure enough *bong* rang out eleven times.

"Perhaps your watch needs a new battery or something, Banger," Mr Grassgrow suggested kindly.

But Banger was too busy banging his watch on the desk and muttering "Stupid thing, stupid thing" to hear.

"Ahem," coughed Peter Purbright. "I think I can hear Madame Estella's poem now," he said. And he began . . .

"Fuzzy Wuzzy was a bear,
Fuzzy Wuzzy had no hair.
He wasn't fuzzy, wuzzy?"

Everyone in the class laughed. Trust Madame Estella to recite something funny.

Then it was Oscar's turn to listen.

"As our newest pupil, Oscar," said Mr Grassgrow. "You must have your hearing tested."

Oscar smiled. That wasn't too terrible. He'd had that done in his last school. Just put the headphones on and listen. Easy.

But this was different.

Mr Grassgrow put a chair in the middle of the floor, facing away from the class

"Will you come and sit in this, please, Oscar," he said. Oscar felt a bit silly, but he sat down.

"Now," said Mr Grassgrow. "Tell me what you hear."

Oscar listened. "I don't hear anything," he said.

"Yes, you do," said Mr Grassgrow. "You're just not listening. What do you hear?"

Oscar listened again.

"I still don't hear anything," he said.

"I'm sure you do, Oscar. Try again."

Oscar listened. The room was quiet. Oscar listened some more. The room was still quiet. Then – wait a minute – Mr Grassgrow was right. He *did* hear things.

"I *can* hear things," he said excitedly.

"What can you hear, Oscar?"

"I can hear the number nine bus."

"Good. How do you know it's the number nine?"

"It's the only one that stops outside the school gate."

"Yes, what else?"

"I can hear Banger's desk creak."

"Good. How do you know it's Banger's desk?"

"Because he's always banging about and never sits still."

Banger scowled.

"What else?"

"I can hear Wibbly's got the burps."

"How do you know that?"

"Because he told me his mum ran out of milk this morning and he had to put Coke over his cornflakes"

"Very good indeed, Oscar," beamed Mr Grassgrow. "You obviously don't have extra-acute hearing, but you listened very intelligently and that's just as important at S.O.G.G.Y."

The class all cheered. All, that is, except Banger McGrath. He sat very still at his desk trying not to bang about or creak. He didn't want to make Hover Boy any more popular than he was.

"And why," he muttered to himself, "didn't I think of any of those things when it was *my* hearing test?"

CHAPTER SEVEN

The three friends didn't manage to meet in their favourite spot by the oak tree for the rest of that day. Banger wouldn't let them. He stuck to their heels like dog poo and they couldn't shake him off. Oscar only just managed to whisper, "The caravan den after tea tonight," before Banger pushed in and demanded to know what they were talking about.

"We're not talking about anything," said Gnatalie.

"Only idiots talk about nothing," sneered Banger.

"Well, you should know," replied

Oscar. Banger made a grab for him, but the faint feeling of fizziness started in Oscar's feet and lifted him off the ground. Banger fell on his face on the muddy grass.

"I'll get you for that, Oscar Smith," he yelled. But Oscar just smiled and waved.

He wasn't smiling, though, when he discovered Banger following him home that day. He wasn't sure at first. He just had a feeling, though when he looked round there was no one there. But the feeling wouldn't go away, and one time he turned round so quickly he managed to catch sight of Banger dodging into a doorway.

"Right," said Oscar. "That's it."

He was just going to walk back and have a word with Banger when he saw Evie and Angie, standing outside their favourite shop. They went in there every Saturday with their pocket money and came home with hair colour and body glitter and eye make-up. Evie and Angie were admiring the colour of the latest lipstick when Oscar panted over.

"I need you to do me a favour," he said. "Don't look round."

Evie and Angie immediately looked round. "What is it?"

"I'm being followed by Banger McGrath and I want to shake him off.

64

Will you help?"

"How much?" said the twins.

"I'll buy you that new lipstick
next Saturday."

"Done. What do you want us to do?"

Oscar whispered to them and the
twins giggled.

"Oh, we can do that, no problem."

Oscar and the twins went into the
shop. Oscar immediately hid behind
a rack of multi-coloured T-shirts.
He watched Banger slide in. Then he
watched Banger grow pale as the twins
grabbed him by the arms.

"We know *you*," they said. "You're
Oscar's friend, Banger McGrath.
You're just the person we need. With
your good taste in clothes – we love
your uniform, it used to be your dad's,
didn't it? – we need you to tell us which
skirts and tops will go best with our hair.
Do you think this pink goes with this

purple? Or what about the lime green with the pale blue?"

Oscar grinned as Banger's face got pinker and pinker – and, as he slipped out of the shop he could hear Angie say, "What do you think of this new lipstick, Banger? Would you wear it with the pink or the green?"

Oscar hid in the toy shop next door and watched as Banger rushed out into the street – his face scarlet.

The twins strolled arm in arm out of the shop.

"That's two lipsticks you owe us on Saturday," they said to Oscar.

"One," said Oscar.

"One each," said the twins. "You surely don't expect us to share?"

CHAPTER EIGHT

Gnatalie and Wibbly arrived at the caravan den at seven o'clock. Oscar hovered up and down anxiously as they discussed Boris McGrath's threat to close the school.

"We can't let him do it," said Oscar. "I think we have all been given special gifts for a reason, so we must keep the school open to learn all we can about them. Somehow we must convince Banger's dad that Banger is starting to learn special gifts too."

"But how?" said Gnatalie. "He's hopeless."

"Worse than useless," said Wibbly.

"I know," worried Oscar.

Gnatalie thought for a bit, then said, "When Banger's about, I could call you two and you could pretend not to hear. That way Banger might think he's developing extra-acute hearing."

"Or," said Wibbly, "we could slow down when Banger's chasing us so he thinks he developing super running skills."

"Or," said Oscar, "whenever Banger says anything we could say, 'What a good idea. Why didn't we think of that?' Then he might think he's developing super brain power."

The friends sat back and smiled at each other.

"It's a start," said Oscar. "But how on earth are we going to make him think he's got x-ray vision, mind reading skills *and* that he can hover in the air. That's going to be trickier."

69

Oscar was still racking his brains when Madame Estella made a special announcement at the next school assembly. Usually assemblies were happy occasions. Madame Estella told everyone how well they were doing and how pleased she was with them. Even if she had something to complain about, like litter in the playground, she would say, "Yesterday, Mr Periwinkle found some lost crisp packets in the playground. Please try not to lose any more if you can help it." And those who had dropped the litter would blush and look at their toes. No one liked to upset Madame Estella. No one, that is, except Banger McGrath and his dad.

"I have to announce," said Madame Estella, a little frown creasing her forehead, "that Mr Boris McGrath is going to make a school inspection at

the end of term. It's a special
inspection to make sure we're all
doing our very best. As you know, Mr
McGrath owns the school and takes a
very keen interest in its progress. I'm
sure you will all do brilliantly and show
him how well you are getting on."

Oh no, thought Oscar. I bet
he's told Madame Estella he's thinking
about closing the school. It won't
matter how well we're getting on if
Banger's hopeless, and the inspection
is bound to show that up.

Gnatalie and Wibbly looked at
Oscar. He didn't need Wibbly's mind-
reading powers to know they were
thinking exactly the same thing.

Then Madame Estella made
another announcement.

"I've been worrying," she said,
"about all the homeless people in this
wet weather, and I think that S.O.G.G.Y.

should do something to help. I know we haven't done much in the community in the past, but perhaps it's time to change that. Time to let people know a little about us and about what we do here.

"I've decided, therefore, that we should have a school Extravaganza to raise some money for the homeless shelter. Each person can do their own thing or they can join in with their friends or get their parents to help. It's up to you. I've already decided what I'm going to do, but I can't tell you." She giggled. "It's a surprise. And to allow you to prepare, for one week before there will be," she paused dramatically, "no homework!"

The cheer nearly took the leaky roof off the school. Trust Madame Estella to come up with something to cheer everyone up, especially after the inspection announcement.

But now Oscar had
two things to worry about – saving the
school and coming up with a good
idea for the Extravaganza. Something
that would make money.

It was easy for Gnatalie.

"I'll do some x-ray vision sessions
and I'll get Mum and Dad to make
some sculptures," she said. "If we
give them odd names like Essence
of Donkey or Midnight Cauliflower
they're sure to sell well. I'll get them
to make an appearance, too. That's

73

bound to bring in the crowds."

It was easy for Wibbly too.

"I'll do some mind-reading sessions and I'll get mum to make some of her exotic casseroles to sell. She'll come along too. Ever since she's been on telly people want her autograph. Perhaps we could charge for her autograph and make more money for the shelter. What about you, Oscar, what will you do?"

"Dunno," said Oscar. "I can't really tell when I'm going to hover, so it's tricky. I'll have to think about it." But, just for the moment, he couldn't think of anything he could do. Dad worked in a dairy. Mum worked part-time in the supermarket. He couldn't see how that could help to raise any money. As for the twins, who would pay money to see *them*?

Oscar sighed. Sometimes life was just one big problem after another. He was just having a nibble at his fingernail

when he felt a presence by his right
foot. The presence leaned against his
leg. It was Mystic Mog. She looked up at
him with her unblinking green stare.

"Follow me," he thought she said,
but there was so much noise with the
clattering of chairs as that it was
difficult to be sure. He followed her
anyway.

She led him to her favourite spot
at the top the school steps. Oscar
looked anxiously behind but no one
saw them go. Gnatalie and Wibbly
were admiring the large pot plant
Wanda had grown specially for that
morning's assembly. Yesterday it
had been a small Busy Lizzie; today
it would have looked more at home
in the jungle. And Banger had been
cornered by Miss Twitching enquiring
about his Maths homework.

"Sit down, Oscar," said Mystic Mog.

"It's safe for the moment."

"You really *can* talk," breathed Oscar, for this time there was no other noise to hide it. "I wasn't sure."

"I don't talk to everyone," said Mystic Mog, licking her paws delicately. "And, for the moment, you must keep my secret as best you can, but you must know that the future of the school rests in your hands."

Oscar gulped. "But I don't know how . . . I mean I can't think . . ."

"I will help you all I can," said Mystic Mog. "The school Extravaganza will give you a better chance. That's why I suggested it to Madame Estella."

"She knows?"

"Of course she knows I can talk. Now, pay attention. This Extravaganza is a bit risky. It will publicize the school. It will publicize you. The other  children can hide their gifts more easily than you, but Madame Estella thinks your best chance of leading a happy life is for people to know about your hovering. To know that you will use it to help them, if you can. Madame Estella is convinced that is why the special gifts have been given.

"The Extravaganza must be a big success. It must get so much wonderful publicity that Mr Boris McGrath will not dare close down the school. Of course you must convince him that Banger is learning special gifts, too, or there won't even be an Extravaganza. So it's up to you. I can help you no more."

CHAPTER NINE

Evie and Angie were delighted to hear about the S.O.G.G.Y. Extravaganza.

"At last we'll get to see inside that crazy school of yours. I bet it's got cobwebs hanging from every corner," said Evie.

"And real skeletons in every cupboard," giggled Angie.

"Weird," they both said. "And why an Extravaganza? Why can't you just have a school fair like everyone else with Guess the name of the teddy, pin the tail on the donkey, terrible tea and soggy sandwiches."

"*Soggy sandwiches!*" cried Oscar.

"That's it. That's the answer." And
he shot up into the air and began
hovering excitedly round the room.
Unfortunately he hovered too near
the sitting-room door and his mum
came through and knocked him over.

"Oh, Oscar," she sighed, rubbing
the bump on his forehead. "You know
you shouldn't hover behind doors.
You know how dangerous it is."

"*He's* dangerous," said Evie.
"Hovering about like a, like a—"

"Like a Hover Boy," said Angie.
"Are you going to be hovering at this Extravaganza?"

"Don't know," said Oscar. "Everyone has to do something. Gnatalie's asking her mum and dad to make sculptures and Wibbly's mum will make exotic casseroles."

"What would you like us to do, Oscar?" asked his mum and dad.
"We could help out, too."

"And us," said the twins.

"Er, em – don't know what you could do," said Oscar, going a bit red.

"I know we're not much good at sculptures or exotic casseroles," said his mum, "but we can still help."

"How?" said Oscar.

"Oh, we'll think of something. Something that will raise money for the shelter."

"We've thought of something already," said Evie and Angie who'd been whispering to each other.

"What?" said Oscar.

"Just wait and see," said the twins. "It'll be brilliant."

But not as brilliant as my idea, thought Oscar and couldn't wait to tell Gnatalie and Wibbly.

He got his chance next day. Miss Twitching had insisted Banger catch up with his homework at lunchtime so the friends were free to go to their favourite spot in the school gardens.

They carefully picked their way through the secret path round the bramble patch and came out at the fallen oak tree. They sat down and took out their lunch boxes. As usual, Gnatalie and Oscar shared theirs with

Wibbly. As usual he had a very strange filling in his sandwiches. He was about to feed them to the crows when Oscar stopped him.

"What's in your sandwiches today, Wibbly?"

Wibbly peeled back the soggy bread.

"Who knows," he said. "It could be anything."

The three friends looked at the sandwich filling. There was some purple curly stuff.

"Permed lettuce," said Gnatalie.

Some pale green squidgy stuff.

"Avocado sick," suggested Wibbly.

And some small brown lumps.

"Definitely reindeer droppings," said Oscar. "The sandwiches look really disgusting, but I know just how we can use them. I have a plan that might help save the school. Stage One: when Banger's hanging around us we'll discuss how the soggy sandwiches help us with our special gifts. Banger's bound to think they are *school* sandwiches and want some. We can let him have them all and convince him they're helping him gain special gifts."

"Brilliant idea," said Gnatalie and Wibbly. "Then what?"

"Then," said Oscar, "we go on to Stage Two, and for that we need a small wooden box and some sherbet . . ."

CHAPTER TEN

Stage One was easily carried out. Gnatalie, Wibbly and Oscar talked and talked about how good soggy sandwiches were for improving their special gifts. Next day, Banger pinched them.

"I'm the head boy," he sneered. "I can take anything I want."

"Big bully," said the three friends, trying not to giggle. Banger ran away laughing, but not for long.

Shortly afterwards they saw him in the playground looking a bit sick. "What was in those sandwiches?" he asked.

"Not sure," said Wibbly truthfully.

"They tasted strange," said Banger.

"That must mean they're working," said Oscar.

"How soon will I know?"

The friends looked at each other. "You must eat them for about a week," they said.

Banger looked even sicker and turned away.

"Now for Stage Two," said Oscar. "Gnatalie, can you get your mum and dad to make a small wooden box with glass on one side and a sliding wooden panel – something like this." And he showed her a drawing.

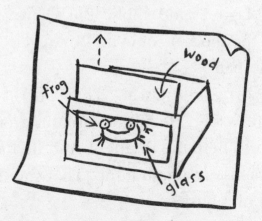

"No problem," said Gnatalie "but what for?"

"So that we can fool Banger into thinking he's got x-ray vision."

"Good thinking, Hover Boy," grinned Gnatalie.

"But what about the mind-reading?" said Wibbly. "Banger couldn't read your mind if it was written on your forehead."

"He doesn't have to," said Oscar. "Whenever he says anything, say: 'I was just thinking that. You must be a mind reader.' He'll be too pleased with himself to be suspicious."

"Magic," said Wibbly. "But where does the sherbet come in. Do we get to eat that?"

"Sorry," said Oscar. "That's for Banger's feet. He has to rub it in every night to help the fizziness. And he has to practise the high jump. That should keep him busy."

Stage Two was ready to put into operation one week later. The friends met in their caravan den to look at the small wooden box Gnatalie's dad had made. It was exactly like Oscar's drawing with glass on one side and a sliding wooden panel.

Oscar took the box and planted a green plastic frog inside.

"When Banger appears," he said, "I'll pretend to be testing your x-ray vision. I'll hold the wooden panel side towards you two, then I'll slide it back and show the glass side to Banger. Hey presto, he'll see the frog."

"Brilliant," said Gnatalie and Wibbly.

"I hope so," said Oscar, and crossed his fingers and his eyes. He would have crossed his toes, too, but the faint feeling of fizziness had started in them, and a moment later he bumped his

87

head on the caravan roof.

"I'm going to start wearing a crash helmet soon," he muttered.

Banger wasn't enjoying Wibbly's sandwiches at all.

"Are you sure these are special S.O.G.G.Y. sandwiches?" he said in school next day. "How do I know they're really working? How do I know I'm learning special gifts? How do I know you three haven't just made all this up?"

"I was just thinking the same, Banger," said Oscar.

"So was I," said Gnatalie.

"Me too," said Wibbly.

"I think it's time you put the sandwiches to the test, Banger. It's only fair. After lunch tomorrow when you've eaten up every last crumb of the soggy sandwiches we'll carry out an x-ray vision test. What do you think about that?"

"I think it's a good idea," muttered Banger.

"I was just thinking that too," said Gnatalie.

"That's funny, so was I," said Wibbly.

"What about the hovering?" said Banger. "My dad wants me to do that. When can we test for that?"

"I was coming to that," said Oscar. "You must have read my mind, Banger. Tomorrow I will bring in the special white powder for your feet."

"White powder? What's this about white powder? You never said anything in class about white powder."

Oscar shrugged. "I didn't want to give away all my secrets. You must rub the white powder into your feet at night. Then when they're covered, plunge your feet into ice-cold water. If the water fizzes, the powder is starting to work. After that it's just a matter of time. That, and lunchtime high jump practices."

"What for?" said Banger. "I hate P.E."

"To improve your hovering height," said Oscar. "No point in hovering only two centimetres above the ground. Who's going to notice that?"

CHAPTER ELEVEN

Oscar could think of nothing else next morning except the test for Banger, so his mind really wasn't on his work. The first discovery was a new one called "How much can you remember?".

Ollie Thomson, a plump little boy from a younger class, came in to talk about his fantastic photographic memory. Mr Blister sat him on a chair facing the class and asked him how it worked.

Ollie blinked several times at the class and said, "I'm really not sure. I just know I can look at a page of a book and immediately it seems to go into my brain and I can then repeat what the page says. My mum sends me for the shopping a lot."

Mr Blister smiled. "I'm going to project a page from the dictionary on to the wall and give everyone two minutes to memorize what they can. Then we'll check the results against what Ollie can remember."

Mr Blister fiddled with the projector for a moment, then the page appeared. Upside down.

Mr Blister muttered.

"We could all stand on our heads," giggled Peter Purbright, otherwise known as Big-ears because of his extra-acute hearing.

"I heard that," said Mr Blister and fixed the page the tight way up.

Oscar looked at the wall. He'd never seen so many words. They started at "clog dance" and ended at "cloth cap".

And there were all the definitions
of the words in between. It was mind-
boggling. I'll never remember any
of this, thought Oscar.

After two minutes Mr Blister
switched off the projector and asked
Ollie to recite what he could remember.
He was word perfect. Not a word or a
definition missed out.

Mr Blister asked the rest of the
class. They weren't very good but no
one was as bad as Oscar who could
only remember, "Close down: To stop
or cease operations entirely."

Banger smirked. He was pretty sure
he knew what was in Oscar's mind.

Later that morning, in the Language
discovery, Oscar said Brussels was
famous for its sprouts. In Science, he
said a little insect with a hundred legs
was called a centimetre, and in History,
he said Napoleon was a brandy his dad

liked. His teachers all thought he was being very silly, so he was really glad when lunchtime came, and he could put Stage Two into operation.

Gnatalie, Wibbly and Oscar gathered at the front door and sat on the school steps beside Mystic Mog to watch Banger finish every last crumb of Wibbly's sandwiches. Banger gulped and swallowed, gulped and swallowed, till they were all eaten. Then Oscar reached into his rucksack and took out the wooden box.

"Now," he said to Banger. "We'll do this test scientifically. Gnatalie will look through the side of this box. She will say nothing, but will write down what she sees." And, like a magician he showed Gnatalie the box, wooden side out.

Gnatalie wrote, "I see a grene plastick frog in the box."

Then Oscar showed the box – wooden side out – to Wibbly.

Wibbly wrote down, "I can't see anything at all in the box."

Then Oscar secretly flipped away the wooden slide and showed Banger the glass side of the box.

Banger's eyes grew wide with excitement and he wrote down quickly. "I see a green plarstic fwog in the box."

"Now," said Oscar, desperately trying to keep a straight face, "we will compare the results of this scientific experiment."

He held up Wibbly's paper.

"Wibbly can see nothing in the box," said Oscar.

He held up Gnatalie's paper.

"Gnatalie can see a green plastic frog in the box."

He held up Banger's paper.

"Banger can also see a green plastic

frog in the box."

And from the box Oscar dramatically drew out a green plastic frog. *Ta da!*

Banger danced up and down on the steps. "They're working. They're working. The soggy sandwiches are horrible, but they're working. I've got x-ray vision. I have. I have."

"But it might not always work, Banger," warned Gnatalie. "Don't expect it to happen all the time. Give your eyes a rest sometimes."

But Banger wasn't listening. He was keen to gain more special powers. "What about that special white powder you told me about?" he said. "Have you brought that?"

Oscar handed over the sherbet powder in a plain white bag.

"I can't wait to try it," said Banger and hurried off.

Oscar grinned. "Stage Two complete," he said, and stroked Mystic Mog's head. She said nothing but Oscar was sure he saw her wink.

CHAPTER TWELVE

School inspection day arrived, and with it a large silver Rolls-Royce. It drew up outside the school and Banger's dad got out. He wore a navy and yellow pinstriped suit and a red tie. The navy and yellow suit strained across his huge frame, and a large diamond in his tie pin tried to outwink the one in his gold tooth. He carried a heavy leather briefcase chained to his wrist.

Madame Estella went to meet him.

"Good morning, Mr McGrath," she said. "The school is ready for your inspection."

And it was. They'd been getting it ready for weeks.

Desks were tidied up, cupboards were tidied out, even Fred, the skeleton, had had a wash and brush. The children's work was pinned up on the walls, and homework notebooks were left out for inspection, especially Banger's, who'd finally caught up with his Maths. But Banger's dad wasn't interested in any of that. He hardly gave any of it a passing glance.

"What I want to know," he said to Madame Estella, "is Boris Junior really learning any special gifts. Gifts that will be useful to me. I mean gifts that will be useful to *him*, in later life. He tells me he is learning some."

"Well," said Madame Estella, "Banger certainly feels he is making progress. He has been working very hard in the gym recently. I think he may well be our high jump champion this year."

"High jump champion," Mr McGrath stroked his chins. "I didn't know he was good at that. If he practised hard enough he could be an Olympic gold medallist. They can make a lot of money. Keep him at it, Madame Estella. Maybe I won't close down this school just yet. Maybe it will make me some money after all. But I shall be keeping a close eye on it and on the progress of

Boris Junior. I want to see results."
And he headed back towards the
front door.

"But don't you want to see more
of what the children are doing?"
asked Madame Estella. "And I wanted
to speak to you about the leaky roof."

"No time. No time. Time is money.
Time is money. I must go." And he lit
a fat cigar and waddled back to his
Rolls.

CHAPTER THIRTEEN

Everyone breathed a sigh of relief
that the so-called inspection was over –
at least for the time being.

"All that time tidying desks he
didn't even look at," muttered Gnatalie.

"And pinning stuff on the walls,"
muttered Wibbly.

"And listening out for his Rolls-
Royce," muttered Big-ears.

"To say nothing of growing all these
plants to make the school look nice,"
scowled Wanda. "I'm exhausted."

They all glared at Banger who
just smirked and said. "My dad can
do anything he likes, so there."

*   *   *

Next there was the Extravaganza to prepare for.

"I can't believe it's tomorrow," said Gnatalie. "But the sculptures are all ready. There are four of them. Spring, Summer, Autumn and Winter. It's easy to tell which is which. Half my clothes have disappeared into them. My T-shirt with the lambs has gone into the Spring one. My swimsuit is hanging from the Summer one. My brown sweater is part of the Autumn one, and I can't find my bobble hat anywhere. I expect it's in the Winter one somewhere."

"We've got loads of exotic casseroles in the freezer too," said Wibbly. "Mum's been working hard."

Oscar said nothing. He just worried. He knew the Extravaganza had to be a big success. He knew the fate of the school could depend on that. He knew

Mystic Mog was depending on him.
What he didn't know was whether he
would be able to hover when the time
came, or even what his mum and dad
were doing to help. They had been
whispering together and nodding and
winking. They were being as mysterious
as the twins. It was very worrying.

Madame Estella had asked Oscar
if he would try to hover by the school
door on Extravaganza day and direct
people into the hall.

"They'll just love to see you hover,
Oscar," she said. "You'll be a star
attraction."

Oscar arrived early to make sure
everything was in order. Gnatalie's
mum and dad arrived soon after with
their sculptures. They looked as
interesting as the sculptures themselves.
They were dressed in grubby denims
with paint splodges all over them and

they obviously didn't wash much.

"Soap dodgers I call them," muttered Gnatalie. "And it's supposed to be children who don't like washing."

Wibbly's mum arrived next with her exotic casseroles. They all had strange names like Taste Bud Tingle or Tongues in Tangle, even Mouthwatering Melange.

"Which means mouthwatering mixture, if you don't speak cooking," explained Wibbly.

Wibbly's mum looked exotic, too.

"I like her red hair," said Oscar.

"A wig," said Wibbly.

"I like her green eyes."

"Contact lenses," said Wibbly.

"I like her purple nails."

"Same colour as the kitchen walls," said Wibbly.

"Cool," said Oscar.

"But not as cool as your mum and dad," said Wibbly. "Look!"

Oscar looked and looked again. His mum and dad had come into the hall wearing very white trousers and T-shirts. On the T-shirts it said, "Get in the moo-d. Have a milkshake." And they were both pushing a large milkshake machine.

"The dairy let me borrow it," said his dad, "since it's for a good cause."

"And the supermarket donated the milk and all the flavourings," beamed his mum.

"Wow," said Oscar, and was just getting over his surprise when the twins came in lugging a large suitcase.

"What on earth—" said Oscar.

The twins heaved the suitcase on to a table and opened it.

"Introducing," they said, "Evie and Angie's beauty school! We'll do make-up, face paints, spray-on hair colour, nail polish and stick-on tattoos – anything to do with beauty."

"What a great idea," said Gnatalie, before Oscar could protest. "How much for a stick-on tiger tattoo?"

"You mean people will pay you for this?" gasped Oscar.

"Just wait and see," said the twins.

Soon the school hall was filled to overflowing with people enjoying the

Extravaganza. They were amazed to see Oscar hovering by the door.

"How does he do it?" they asked. "Is it a trick? He should be on the telly. Bet he gets a good view at football matches."

Oscar just grinned and showed more people into the hall. Hovering above everyone else, he was able to direct people to the various stalls, and hold lost children above his head till they found their mums.

"Isn't it wonderful, Oscar," said Madame Estella, who was dressed up as Madame Claire Voyant, the famous fortune teller, for the day. "Just think of the money we'll be able to give to the shelter. Aren't your parents and your sisters fantastic? You must be very proud of them."

"I am," grinned Oscar.

"And a little bird, or at least a little cat, told me what you'd been up to with

Banger. That was very clever, if a bit naughty, and it has pleased Banger's dad. Thank you for your help."

Oscar blushed and hovered even higher into the air.

"It was nothing," he said. "Now I've just got to go and hover round to make sure no one else gets lost."

The Extravaganza was a real success. Gnatalie's x-ray vision stall drew a great crowd, and Wibbly's mind-reading had folks laughing when he told them they were wondering if they'd left the gas on or if they'd win the lottery.

Wanda Fonda made lots of money at her plant stall as people staggered away with giant geraniums. But Oscar's hovering was the star attraction. People stood and stared at him in amazement, so Oscar felt he couldn't just hover there. He had to do something.

At first he just hovered up and down a bit. Then he became more adventurous and did a little mid air dance. This got so much applause he tried a forward roll, but the faint feeling of fizziness disappeared in the middle of it and he landed, feet first, on Banger McGrath, who was eating a large ice cream at the

time. This got the biggest applause
of all. Oscar got up and bowed.
Banger got up and spluttered.

"I'll get you for that, Hover Boy,"
muttered Banger.

But Oscar didn't care. His
hovering was out in the open and
people liked it. People liked him.

Photos of the extraordinary
Extravaganza and Oscar were all over
the newspapers, and Mr Boris
McGrath, local businessman, was
hailed as the great benefactor of the
shelter and of the School Of Greatly
Gifted Youth. There was even a
photograph of him with his hand on
Banger's shoulder, trying to look kindly.
There was no way he could easily close
the school now.

Gnatalie, Wibbly and Oscar pored
over the papers in their caravan den.

"There's you with your hair

sprayed green, Gnatalie," laughed Oscar. "And you, Wibbly, with your nose in a banana milkshake."

"And look at you, Oscar," they said, "hovering around looking very pleased about everything. And so you should. You saved the school, Hover Boy."

Oscar smiled and turned pink.

"It was nothing," he muttered.

But it was *everything*. Oscar was really happy at S.O.G.G.Y. Happy with his friends, happy with his teachers. Banger McGrath and his father were a problem, but so far he had managed to deal with it.

"We all helped save the school," said Oscar. "And for that I think we deserve a little reward. We've still got the milkshake machine in the garden shed, who's for a strawberry one?"